To the memory of Barbara Tacy, who loved horses of many colors
—J. Y.

To Alice and Mona. With love.
—J. D.

SIMON SPOTLIGHT
An imprint of Simon & Schuster Children's Publishing Division
1230 Avenue of the Americas, New York, New York 10020
This Simon Spotlight edition December 2022
Text copyright © 2022 by Jane Yolen
Illustrations copyright © 2022 by Joëlle Dreidemy
For information about special discounts for bulk purchases, please contact Simon & Schuster
Special Sales at 1-866-506-1949 or business@simonandschuster.com.
Manufactured in the United States of America 1122 LAK
10 9 8 7 6 5 4 3 2 1
Library of Congress Cataloging-in-Publication Data
Names: Yolen, Jane, author. | Dreidemy, Joëlle, illustrator.
Title: Interrupting Cow and the horse of a different color / by Jane Yolen;
illustrated by Joëlle Dreidemy.
Description: Simon Spotlight edition. | New York, New York : Simon
Spotlight, [2022] | Series: Interrupting Cow | Audience: Ages 5–7. |
Summary: Cow meets a new friend on the farm, Zebra, who knows a lot of jokes
and all about the big bright world beyond the farm.
Identifiers: LCCN 2022035049 (print) | LCCN 2022035050 (ebook) | ISBN
9781665914390 (paperback) | ISBN 9781665914406 (hardcover) | ISBN
9781665914413 (ebook)
Subjects: CYAC: Jokes—Fiction. | Cows—Fiction. | Zebras—Fiction. |
Friendship—Fiction. | Humorous stories. | LCGFT: Humorous fiction. |
Picture books.
Classification: LCC PZ7.Y78 Il 2022 (print) | LCC PZ7.Y78 (ebook) |
DDC [E]—dc23
LC record available at https://lccn.loc.gov/2022035049
LC ebook record available at https://lccn.loc.gov/2022035050

INTERRUPTING COW

and the HORSE of a DIFFERENT COLOR

by JANE YOLEN
illustrated by JOËLLE DREIDEMY

Ready-to-Read

Simon Spotlight

New York   London   Toronto   Sydney   New Delhi

Morning did not begin well.
From the horses' side of the barn
came screams and wild neighing.

Interrupting Cow fell out
of a wonderful dream
of hilarious jokes and
munching on sweet grass,
into the sounds of hooves
pounding on the ground.

"Knock, knock," she called out,
hoping to calm things.
Whatever the problem was,
jokes could do that.
Even uninvited ones.

But she was talking to the back ends
of all the other cows
and the horses as well
as they fled the barn in disgust.
None of them liked her jokes.

"Knock, knock," Interrupting Cow
said again, but only to herself.
Telling a joke always made her
feel better.
But before she could get any further,
she heard a single horse crying.
Or maybe, she thought,
not exactly a horse.

It was not as *hoarse* as horses normally were.

She smiled at that little play on words and walked quickly to the horse side of the barn to see what was going on.

There she found a sort-of horse.
Well, at least it was horse shaped,
with slim legs and hooves.
It had horse ears and a long nose,
just like the other horses.

But though she knew white horses
and golden horses, brown, gray,
and black horses, horses with spots
and dots on their skin, this was
definitely a horse of a different color.

"Gosh," said Interrupting Cow to the horse, "you are black stripes on white."

Then she took a closer look. "Or maybe you are white stripes on black."

She got so close to him, her nose touched his skin. "But you still smell like a horse."

And then she remembered another joke . . .
one her father used to tell.
"What's black and white
and read all over?"
"I am not red anywhere,"
the horse said, sniffling sadly.

The horse had a funny way of talking, as if each word took a long time making its way past his black-on-white throat.
Or a white-on-black throat, thought Interrupting Cow. The horse certainly didn't seem to understand her joke, so she explained it with care.

"The answer is not you—
whatever you are.
The answer to 'what is black and white
and read all over' is a newspaper!
Read, *red*—get it?" She fell on the floor
in hopeless laughter.

The horse of a different color
shook his head.
"I still do not understand this joke.
Newspapers are not the color red,
not a bit, and certainly not red
all over. They are black print
on white paper. A bit like me."

"Silly creature," Interrupting Cow said. "Newspapers are read all over the world. Not *red* the color, but *read* as in *reading*."

The horse of a different color neighed,
which sounded a bit like a cough,
and said, "A joke that has to be explained
is a bad joke."
But he was giggling all the same.

"Read and red," he said again.
"If I am a newspaper, I am read.
Not the color red. But I am not a
newspaper. Aha!"

"What are you, then?" he asked.
"I am just an ordinary cow,"
Interrupting Cow said.
"I think not so ordinary," he replied.
"You are kind and funny and very
smart. And I ask you to be my friend."

"And you are . . . ?" she asked.
"I am a zebra," he said.

"Knock, knock!" said
Interrupting Cow.

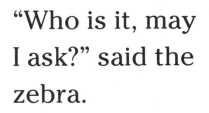

"Who is it, may
I ask?" said the
zebra.

She was so astonished by his asking,
she almost forgot the joke.
But finally, she said, "Interrupting Cow."

He had a funny twinkle in his eye.
"Interrupting Cow wh—"

"Moo!" they said together.

Then they both fell down on the sandy floor of the barn giggling helplessly, their hind feet knocking together, sounding almost like clapping.

When they both recovered,
they stood up and walked out
of the barn.
They were so busy talking,
they did not see the astonished stares
of the other cows and horses.
They did not see the ducks swimming
fast to the other side of the pond,
leaving a scribble of foam.
Or the goats hiding behind rocks
and trees.

"You knew the joke?"
Interrupting Cow asked.
"I was in a traveling circus,"
Zebra said. "It left me by accident
at the station."

"Is that how you knew the joke?"
she asked.
"It was the ringmaster's favorite,"
said Zebra.

"He was the one who introduced us to the audience with such jokes. They always laughed and applauded, even if they had heard the joke before."

"Does he have more jokes?"
Interrupting Cow asked.
"Many more," Zebra said.
"Will you teach them to me?"
she asked.

"I think Ringmaster is the best one to do that, but first we must find the train tracks," he said.

"I have friends who can help us . . .
friends who love jokes," she said.
"What kind of friends?" Zebra asked.
"A rooster, an old dog, and a Whooo,"
Interrupting Cow answered.
"Whoooo—" he began.
"Moo!" she interrupted.
And they both fell down laughing,
friend with friend.